THE MOUSERY

THE

WRITTEN BY Charlotte Pomerantz

ILLUSTRATED BY Kurt Cyrus

MOUSERY

Gulliver Books • Harcourt, Inc. *San Diego New York London*

www.harcourt.com

Gulliver Books is a registered trademark of Harcourt, Inc.

Library of Congress Cataloging-in-Publication Data
Pomerantz, Charlotte.
The mousery/Charlotte Pomerantz; illustrated by Kurt Cyrus.
p. cm.
"Gulliver Books."
Summary: When four orphan mice ask for shelter at the home of
Sliver and Slice on a cold winter evening, the bad-tempered older mice
finally learn to soften their hearts.
[1. Mice—Fiction. 2. Stories in rhyme.] I. Cyrus, Kurt, ill. II. Title.
PZ8.3.P564Mo 2000
[E]—dc21 99-6116
ISBN 0-15-202304-6

First edition
A C E G H F D B

Printed in Singapore

The display type was set in Heatwave.
The text type was set in Columbus MT.
Printed and bound by Tien Wah Press, Singapore
This book was printed on totally chlorine-free Nymolla Matte Art paper.
Production supervision by Pascha Gerlinger
Designed by Lori McThomas Buley

For Carlos Caribou, Tough Tony,
Dr. Clueless, the Floofster, and Kozmo
—C. P.

For Linnea
—K. C.

Two bad-tempered mice
named Sliver and Slice
lived all alone in a mousery.

They lived all alone
without doorbell or phone,
for they wanted no guests in the mousery.

The fire burned low
with a pitiful glow,
though they had lots of wood in the mousery.

Too gloomy to chat,
they quietly sat,
and spoke hardly a word in the mousery.

Once, a wandering mouse,
without his own house,
asked to stay overnight in the mousery.

Shrieked Sliver and Slice,
"We don't like other mice.
This is not a hotel—it's a mousery!"

Then a neighbor close by
brought a warm cherry pie
one Thanksgiving Day to the mousery,

but Sliver and Slice
just shook their heads twice.
"Don't bring your old pies to the mousery."

When some young mice at play
built a snow mouse one day
with armfuls of new-fallen snow,

Sliver and Slice
yelled, "Go away, mice!
No trespassing. N-O spells *no*!"

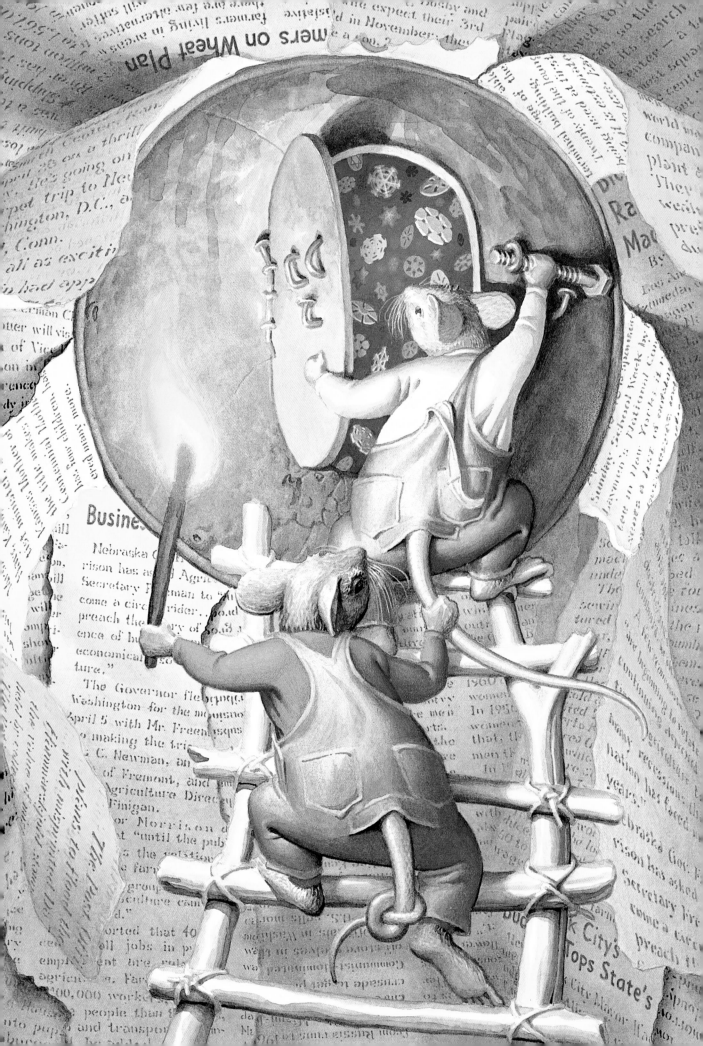

Then one dark, snowy night,
the sky flashed with light.
It was storming as never before.

Said Sliver to Slice,
"Bolt the latch twice.
The wind could blow off the door!"

Just then, through the snow,
in an untidy row,
came four mousekins who squeaked, "Let us in."

"Open up, please.
It's so cold we could freeze!
Our sweaters are ragged and thin."

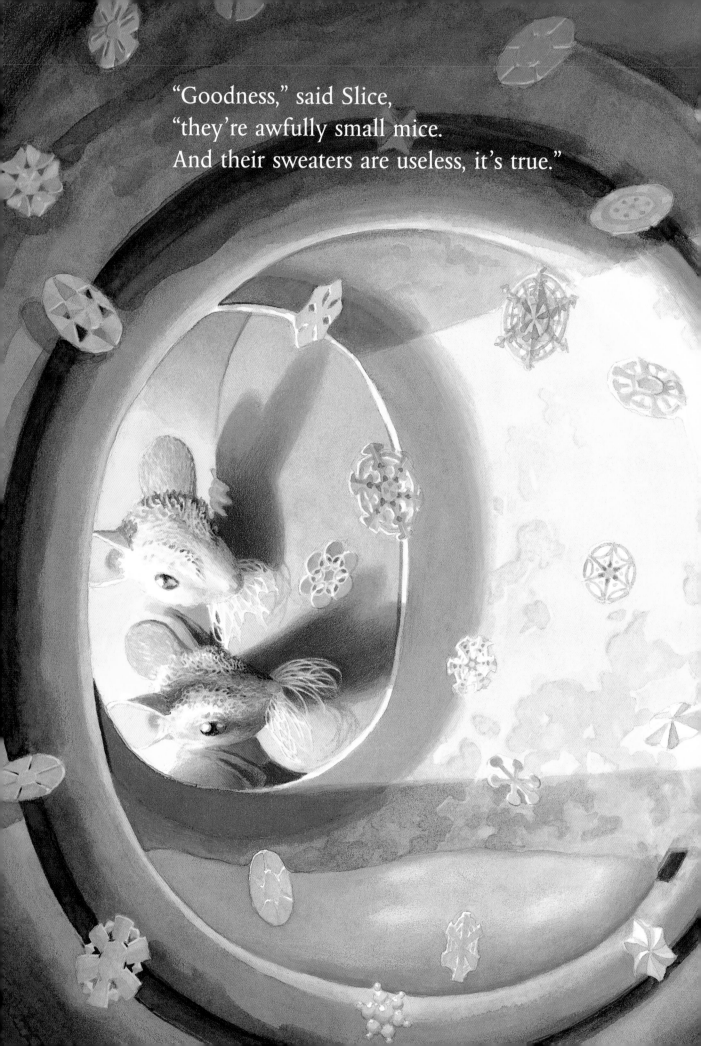

"Goodness," said Slice,
"they're awfully small mice.
And their sweaters are useless, it's true."

"Gracious," said Sliver,
"just look at them shiver.
Their noses are turning quite blue."

So they unlatched the door,
and the wee mousekins four
quietly entered the mousery.

Their eyes opened wide
when they saw the inside
of the roomy but gloomy old mousery.

Squeaked the mousekins, "Good gracious!
This place is so spacious,
but *cold*—it's so cold in this mousery."

As fast as they could,
they fetched kindling and wood
and made a great fire in the mousery.

The four little mice
found brown beans and rice
and cooked them in two iron pots.

Then, adding some spice,
they called Sliver and Slice,
"Come join us! We've made lots and lots."

With a soft chewing sound,
they all sat around
and savored the rice and the beans.

"Sliver," said Slice,
"this is really quite nice.
We're living like kings and like queens."

Then the mousekins made beds,
laid down their wee heads,
and pulled all the blankets up tight.

But though they were warm
from the wind and the storm,
they dreaded the long winter night.

Pit-a-pat…What was that?
They imagined a cat,
lying in wait in the gloom.

Each creak of the door
made them cringe on the floor.
Was the cat—*pit-a-pat*—in the room?

Was that a wolf's howl,
or the hoot of an owl,
waiting outside in the night?

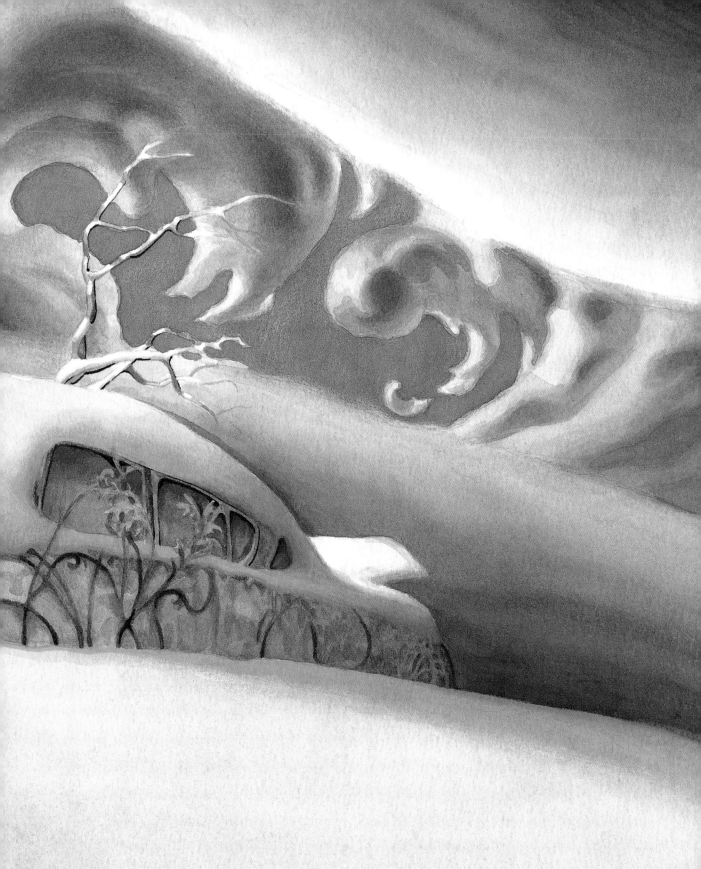

The silence and gloom
of the mousery room
made the wee mousekins quiver with fright.

Then the tiniest sound
floated up from the ground.
A mousekin had started to sing!

Sliver went pale
from his head to his tail,
for the tune had a lullaby ring.

"Slice, am I wrong?
Is that not the same song
that Grandmother sang long ago?"

"Sliver, you're right.
I remember at night
how she sang by the fireside glow."

A sheep has a lambkin,
A duck has a duckling,
And I have a mousekin.
Good night.
A goose has a gosling,
A pig has a suckling,
And I have a mousekin.
Good night.

Hush, it's the hour
When all little babies—
And my little mousekins—
Snuggle up tight and welcome the night.
Good night, little mousekins, good night.

When Sliver and Slice
looked down at the mice,
they heard not a whisper or peep.

The mousekins were dozy,
all warm and all cozy.
One by one they were falling asleep.

How darling they were,
with their soft downy fur,
curled up in an untidy row.

With a yawn and a shiver,
first Slice, and then Sliver,
fell asleep by the fireside glow.

In the morning they woke.
It was Sliver who spoke,
"Slice, do you think we've been wrong?

"They don't fidget or fuss,
and they've been good to us.
I declare they do seem to belong."

Said Slice, "I agree.
I was thinking, you see,
after work, well, perhaps—we could play.

"Though it isn't routine,
if you know what I mean . . .
Why don't we ask them to stay?"

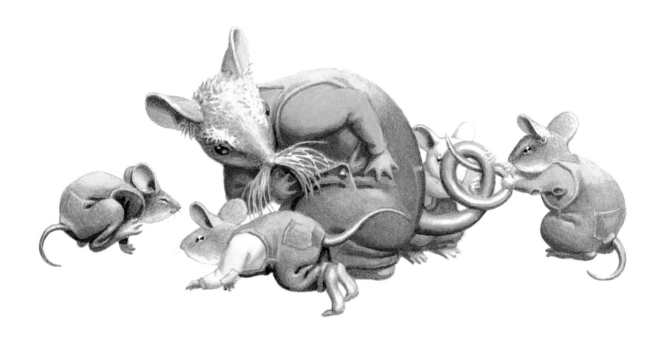

So the four little mice
lived with Sliver and Slice
and scurried all over the mousery.

Sliver and Slice
became fond of *all* mice
and opened the doors of the mousery.

Before very long,
they were fifty-three strong,
running all over the mousery.

With laughter and squeals,
they prepared tasty meals
and baked cherry pies in the mousery.

Outside the house,
they built a snow mouse
from drifts piled high near the door.

There was singing, carousing
in mousery housing,
and laughing as never before!

It was some time ago,
but as far as we know,
to this day, it's the same in the mousery.

And remember the mouse
without his own house,
who was turned away from the mousery?

Well, he passed by one day,
and they all called out, "Hey—
come live with us here in the mousery!"